WRITTEN BY JON SCIESZKA

CHARACTERS AND ENVIRONMENTS DEVELOPED BY THE

DAVID SHANNON   **LOREN LONG**   **DAVID GORDON**

ILLUSTRATION CREW:

Executive producer: ⌐OΓ INDUSTRIES in association with Animagic S.L.

Creative supervisor: Sergio Pablos ○ Drawings by: Juan Pablo Navas ○ Color by: Isabel Nadal

Color assistant: Gabriela Lazbal ○ Art director: Karin Paprocki

READY-TO-ROLL

ALADDIN PAPERBACKS
NEW YORK   LONDON   TORONTO   SYDNEY

ALADDIN PAPERBACKS

An imprint of Simon & Schuster Children's Publishing Division

1230 Avenue of the Americas, New York, NY 10020

The text of this book was set in Truck King.

Manufactured in the United States of America

First Aladdin Paperbacks edition January 2009

10 9 8 7 6

Library of Congress Cataloging-in-Publication Data

Scieszka, Jon.

Uh-oh Max / written by Jon Scieszka ; characters and environments developed by

the Design Garage: David Shannon, Loren Long, David Gordon.—1st Aladdin Paperbacks ed.

p. cm—(Jon Scieszka's Trucktown. Ready-to-roll.)

Summary: When Max gets in trouble after speeding up a ramp, all of his

Trucktown friends try to help out.

ISBN-13: 978-1-4169-4141-5   ISBN-10: 1-4169-4141-X (pbk)

ISBN-13: 978-1-4169-4152-1   ISBN-10: 1-4169-4152-5 (library)

[1. Traffic accidents—Fiction. 2. Trucks—Fiction.] I. Design Garage. II. Title.

PZ7.S41267Uh 2009   [E]—dc22   2007027809

1212 LAK

Max Zooms.

Max **jumps**.

Max flies.

"TO THE
MAX!"

he cheers.

Uh-oh.

Max is stuck.
"Call Jack!" Max shouts.

Jack pushes.
No luck. Max is stuck.

"Call Kat!"
Max shouts.

Kat digs.

No luck. Max is stuck.

"Call Gabby!"

Max shouts.

Gabby talks...

and talks...

and talks.

Really no luck.
Max is **really** stuck.
Who can help?

"Do you want an ice cream?
Do you want an ice cream?
Do you want an ice cream?"

An ice cream won't help.

The Fire Truck twins?

Tow Truck Ted?
Of course!

Ted **hOoks** Max.
Ted **flips** Max.

"Hurray for Ted!"

Max zooms.

Max jumps.